The Place Where You Live
El lugar donde vives

By / Por
James Luna

Illustrations by / Ilustraciones de
Thelma Muraida

Spanish translation by / Traducción al español de
Gabriela Baeza Ventura

PIÑATA BOOKS

Piñata Books
Arte Público Press
Houston, Texas

Publication of *The Place Where You Live* is funded by grants from the City of Houston through the Houston Arts Alliance. We are grateful for their support.

Esta edición de *El lugar donde vives* ha sido subvencionada por la Ciudad de Houston por medio del Houston Arts Alliance. Le agradecemos su apoyo.

Piñata Books are full of surprises!
¡Piñata Books están llenos de sorpresas!

Piñata Books
An Imprint of Arte Público Press
University of Houston
4902 Gulf Fwy, Bldg 19, Rm 100
Houston, Texas 77204-2004

Cover design by / Diseño de la portada por Bryan Dechter

Luna, James.
    The place where you live / by James Luna ; illustrations by Thelma Muraida ; Spanish translation by Gabriela Baeza Ventura = El lugar donde vives / por James Luna ; Ilustraciones por Thelma Muraida ; traducción al español de Gabriela Baeza Ventura.
        p   cm
    Summary: Simple rhyming, repetitive text describes "the place where you live," from the warm and sunny kitchen smelling of tortillas and hot chocolate to the yard, neighbors, school, library and front porch.
    ISBN 978-1-55885-813-8 (alk. paper)
    [1. Stories in rhyme. 2. Home—Fiction. 3. Spanish language materials—Bilingual.] I. Muraida, Thelma, illustrator. II. Ventura, Gabriela Baeza, translator. III. Title.
PZ74.3.L85 2015
[E]—dc23
                                                                                                        2015000892
                                                                                                        CIP

∞ The paper used in this publication meets the requirements of the American National Standard for Permanence of Paper for Printed Library Materials Z39.48-1984.

Printed in Hong Kong in May 2015–August 2015
by Book Art Inc. / Paramount Printing Company Limited
12 11 10 9 8 7 6 5 4 3 2 1

*This book is dedicated to Francisco and Aurora, who made the place
where I lived warm and joyous every day.*

—JL

To Diego, Elias and Avia.

—TM

*Les dedico este libro a Francisco y a Aurora, quienes día a día hicieron del
lugar donde viví un hogar cálido y feliz.*

—JL

Para Diego, Elias y Avia.

—TM

This is the place where you live.

Este es el lugar donde vives.

This is the kitchen, warm and sunny,

with tortillas, hot chocolate and everything yummy,

here in the place where you live.

Esta es la cocina, cálida y soleada,

con tortillas, chocolate caliente y rica comida,

aquí en el lugar donde vives.

This is the garden, alive and green,

with peppers and squash that you planted in spring,

here in the place where you live.

Este es el huerto, vivo y verde,

con los chiles y las calabazas que sembraste en primavera,

aquí en el lugar donde vives.

This is the neighbor who makes sweet cornbread

to trade with Grandma for tortillas instead,

here in the place where you live.

Este es el vecino que hornea pan de maíz

para intercambiarlo por las tortillas de Abuela,

aquí en el lugar donde vives.

This is the store just across the street

with popsicles and gum and all kinds of sweets,

here in the place where you live.

Esta es la tienda al otro lado de la calle

con paletas, chicles y todo tipo de dulces,

aquí en el lugar donde vives.

This is the school where all your friends go

to play at recess and learn and grow,

here in the place where you live.

Esta es la escuela donde van todos tus amigos

a jugar en el recreo y aprender y crecer,

aquí en el lugar donde vives.

This is the library so very quiet

where you read about voyages, magic and giants,

here in the place where you live.

Esta es la biblioteca tan tranquila

donde lees de viajes, magia y gigantes,

aquí en el lugar donde vives.

These are the trees that grow green and tall

with blossoms and fruit and shade for us all,

here in the place where you live.

Estos son los árboles que crecen verdes y altos

con flores y frutas y sombra para todos,

aquí en el lugar donde vives.

This is the field where you play with your team,

and parents cheer and your friends scream,

here in the place where you live.

Esta es la cancha donde juegas con tu equipo,

y los papás celebran y los amigos gritan,

aquí en el lugar donde vives.

This is the park for your family time

where you swing and slide and laugh and climb,

here in the place where you live.

Este es el parque para pasar tiempo con tu familia

donde te columpias y deslizas y ríes y brincas,

aquí en el lugar donde vives.

These are the carts ringing happy bells

with hot corn and snow cones that walking men sell,

here in the place where you live.

Aquí están los carritos que suenan alegres campanas

con hombres que venden elotes calientes y raspas en la calle,

aquí en el lugar donde vives.

These are the lawns with green grass and bright flowers

where you play and you laugh for hours and hours,

here in the place where you live.

Estos son el césped verde y las flores brillantes

donde juegas y ríes por horas y horas,

aquí en el lugar donde vives.

This is the porch here at home

where you sit with your family when the day is done.

This is the place where you live.

Este es el porche aquí en tu hogar

donde te sientas con tu familia al terminar el día.

Este es el lugar donde vives.

These are the arms of your mom and dad

hugging you after the long day you've had.

They love you because you make them so glad,

here in the place where you live.

Estos son los brazos de Mamá y Papá

abrazándote después de un largo día.

Te quieren porque los haces feliz

aquí en el lugar donde vives.

James Luna is the author of a bilingual chapter book for intermediate readers, *A Mummy in Her Backpack / Una momia en su mochila,* and a bilingual picture book, *The Runaway Piggy / El cochinito fugitivo,* which was chosen by Texas schoolchildren as the winner of the 2012 Tejas Star Book Award. The place where James Luna used to live and that inspired this story is San Bernardino, California. The place where he eats candy, cooks and reads is Riverside, California. Visit www.moonstories.com to learn more about him.

James Luna es autor del libro bilingüe para lectores intermedios, *A Mummy in Her Backpack / Una momia en su mochila,* y el libro infantil, *The Runaway Piggy / El cochinito fugitivo,* fue elegido por estudiantes en Texas como ganador del Tejas Star Book Award del 2012. San Bernardino, California, es el lugar que inspiró la historia y en donde vivió James Luna. El lugar en donde come dulces, cocina y lee es Riverside, California. Visita www.moonstories.com para aprender más sobre él.

Thelma Muraida, an accomplished designer and artist, illustrated *Clara and the Curandera / Clara y la curandera* (Piñata Books, 2011), *My Big Sister / Mi Hermana mayor* (Piñata Books, 2012) and Cecilia and *Miguel are Best Friends / Cecilia y Miguel son mejores amigos* (Piñata Books, 2014). She has designed several book covers and illustrated articles for national publications. She currently lives in San Antonio, Texas, with her husband and two dogs. Art, music and dance are always alive in their home, and their three children have appreciated and incorporated them into their lives.

Thelma Muraida, una diseñadora y artista consumada, ilustró *Clara and the Curandera / Clara y la curandera* (Piñata Books, 2011), *My Big Sister / Mi hermana mayor* (Piñata Books, 2012) y Cecilia and *Miguel are Best Friends / Cecilia y Miguel son mejores amigos* (Piñata Books, 2014). Ha diseñado varias portadas de libros e ilustrado artículos para publicaciones nacionales. En la actualidad, vive en San Antonio, Texas, con su esposo y sus dos perros. El arte, la música y el baile siempre están presentes en su hogar, y sus tres hijos los han apreciado e incorporado en sus vidas.